TINY TED'S
WINTER

Peter Bowman

HUTCHINSON

London   Sydney   Auckland   Johannesburg

For Mum, Dad and Lassie

'It's snowing,'
said Mouse…

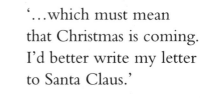

'...which must mean
that Christmas is coming.
I'd better write my letter
to Santa Claus.'

'Robin, will you please take this to Santa?'

'I'll write a letter too.
Now, what would I like?'

'Oh no, I've missed Robin.'

'Never mind,
I'll take it to
Santa myself.
Wheeee!'

'Oops!'

'That was lucky.'

'Sorry, I can't stop. I'm
looking for Santa Claus.'

'Perhaps this is
where he lives.'

'I'll ask inside.'

'Hello, I'm looking
for Santa Claus.'
    'You just missed
him,' said a big bear.

'Oh dear, oh dear.
It's getting dark…
I'd better hurry.'

'Where *is* he? I've looked *everywhere*.'

'One last place to try.

'Ah ha! No presents.
That means he hasn't
been here yet...'

'I'll wait for him to come
down the chimney...'

'Mmm, that was tasty.'

'I think
I'll have
a little nap.'

'Hey! What's happening?'

'Oh no, don't
put me in
the rubbish.'

'Phew! Where am I?'

'Oh dear, I've
lost my letter.
I won't get a
present now.'

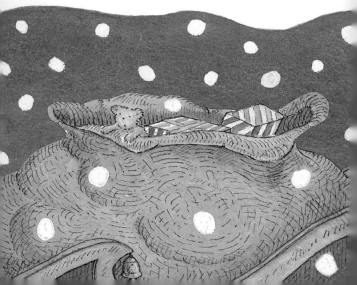

'Where am I *now*?'

'Christmas won't be the same without Tiny Ted,' said Mouse.

'Now, what did Santa bring me…?'

'…TINY TED!'

'I've got a present too,' said Tiny Ted.
'Santa must have got my letter after all!'

First published in 1994

1 3 5 7 9 10 8 6 4 2

© Peter Bowman 1994

Peter Bowman has asserted his right under
the Copyright, Designs and Patents Act, 1988,
to be identified as the author of this work

First published in the United Kingdom in 1994 by
Hutchinson Children's Books
Random House UK Limited
20 Vauxhall Bridge Road, London SW1V 2SA

Random House Australia (Pty) Limited
20 Alfred Street, Milsons Point, Sydney
New South Wales 2061, Australia

Random House New Zealand Limited
18 Poland Road, Glenfield
Auckland 10, New Zealand

Random House South Africa (Pty) Limited
PO Box 337, Bergvlei, South Africa
Random House UK Limited Reg. No. 954009

A CIP catalogue record for this book
is available from the British Library

ISBN: 0 09 176167 0

Printed in China